Knights

Terry Deary

Illustrated by Martin Brown

SCHOLASTIC

For Paul Burdess – Knight of the Road. TD

To Andrew, Elizabeth and everyone at Wimborne library for your
friendly help, the occasional blind eye to a late book and allowing me
to strip the shelves of any given subject. Thanks. MB

Scholastic Children's Books,
Euston House, 24 Eversholt Street,
London, NW1 1DB UK

A division of Scholastic Ltd
London ~ New York ~ Toronto ~ Sydney ~ Auckland
Mexico City ~ New Delhi ~ Hong Kong

First published in the UK by Scholastic Ltd, 2006

13 digit ISBN 978 0439 95577 5

Printed and bound by Tien Wah Press Pte. Ltd, Singapore

4 6 8 10 9 7 5

Contents

Introduction

A knight's job is to kill somebody. To batter, slash, stab, crush, slice or mangle them to a mush.

So there are not a lot of nice knights around in history. Many were bullies and cold-blooded killers — and that was just the pleasant ones. The really rotten ones were murder machines.

Of course there are some lovely fairy tales about knights in shining armour. You know the sort of thing...

If you want stories like that then go to the library. If you want stories like that do NOT read this book!

This is a horrible history of days of old when knights were cold (hearted). The only princesses you'll meet are probably more dead than dead pretty.

This book will tell you the terrible truths. Like:

RICHARD THE LIONHEART WENT ON CRUSADE TO JERUSALEM AND HE HAD THE HEAD OF A SARACEN ENEMY CUT OFF AND CURRIED.[1] HE ATE IT!

URRGGGGHH!

You have been warned! There are some seriously scary bits so do NOT attempt to read it with the lights out. In other words ...

HORRIBLE HISTORIES WARNING:

This book is not for reading by knight[2]!

---

1 Sadly poor Richard could not have chips with his curry as they hadn't been invented.
2 Oh yes, and apart from foul facts about very bad men there may be one or two very bad jokes.

Knight time

Knights are a special sort of soldier, better trained to use better weapons than peasants like you and me.

Where did they come from? Did a warlord wake up one night and say...

No. It just didn't happen like that. The idea grew slowly over hundreds of years – like the mould on a school-dinner pie.

But, every now and then, something b-i-g happened in the world of war. Some small step for a gang of knights but a giant leap for knighthood.

Here are the nasty highlights...

AD 378 Battle of Adrianople (now Edirne in Turkey)
Roman legions smashed in battle by heavily armed Goths (barbarians) on horses. Most of the 40,000 Romans massacred.

The Emperor Valens is wounded and carried to a peasant's cottage to be treated. The Goths find the cottage full of Romans and burn it to the ground.

Monk Saint Ambrose said…

It is the end of the world.

It wasn't. But it would soon be the end for the Roman Empire. It's the start of almost 1,500 years of horrible history for the rampaging riders.

AD 518 Battle of Badon, Britain

Old reports tell of King Arthur's last great battle at Badon Mount. The report says…

> The twelfth battle was on Badon hill and in it nine hundred and sixty men fell in one day, from a single charge of Arthur's and no one lay them low save he alone.

Wow! Arthur killed 960 men himself? No wonder it was his last battle. His arms must have been dropping off after all that chopping!

Some historians say he died at Camlan in 537 – others say he is sleeping in a magical cave. He'll wake up and come to Britain's rescue when the country is in danger.

Hmmmm! You can believe that if you want. Some people do.

1066 Battle of Hastings, Britain

The English (on foot) keep the Norman invaders (on horses) off their hill top all day long. But in the end the Norman knights break through and chop Saxon King Harold into bits. The Normans will make great knights in the future.

1095 First Crusade, Palestine

Pope Urban is upset because those Norman knights are so keen on a scrap they are butchering each other. He says...

Pope Urban tells the Christian knights that the Emperor in Byzantium needs their help. He is being attacked by the Muslim forces. He also mentions that the Holy Land (around Jerusalem) has been taken over by the Muslims. Pope Urban then gives the knights a licence to kill. Sort of 'Kill the enemies of the church and God will let you straight into heaven'.

Instead of a *bit* of help for the Emperor, the Pope gets a *huge* army from Europe. Instead of helping the Emperor, the army launches an invasion. A Crusade.

So the mindless and murderous Crusades start. Will the Christians win? No hope, Pope, you dope.

1099 El Cid dies, Spain

This great Spanish fighter (real name Rodrigo de Bivar) is nicknamed El Cid – The Lord. He has a lion for a pet and is unbeatable in battles against the North African invaders – the Moors. It is said that in one battle he cut down 300 Moors all by himself. Whenever the enemy see him they run away (though that could be something to do with seeing his lion!). Rod has a dream that he will die in 30 days. He leaves orders for his men to fasten his corpse to his warhorse so his body can lead his men into war one last time. The Moors hear that El Cid is dead – when they see the body riding towards them they think he's risen from the dead and run away. Who can blame them?

EL CID? EX CID?

The Spanish can't bear to bury El Cid, so they sit him on a throne for ten years before they put him underground!

1214 Roger Bacon born, England

There are no knights riding into battle in the twenty-first century, are there? Why not?

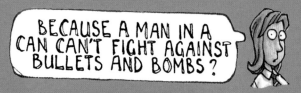

BECAUSE A MAN IN A CAN CAN'T FIGHT AGAINST BULLETS AND BOMBS?

Roger Bacon was a monk. He didn't invent gunpowder – he borrowed the idea from the Chinese who'd had it for hundreds of years. But he brought it to Europe and over time it was used to fire cannon and pistols.

That would mean curtains drawn on knight time.

Roger Bacon tried to make gold from lead and failed, but his experiments with gunpowder worked. So did his experiments on glasses (he wore them) and on light.

So what happened to this marvellous monk?

a) He was made pope for being so clever.

b) He sold his idea for a fortune and made his monastery the richest in the world.

c) He was thrown into prison for ten years.

Answer: c) He made a b-i-g mistake. He argued with the church bosses. THEY said…

THE RAINBOW WAS INVENTED BY GOD SO WE REMEMBER NOAH'S ARK LANDING SAFELY

But Roger argued…

THE RAINBOW IS WHEN WATER BENDS LIGHT. SEE! GOD DIDN'T COME INTO IT

Bacon was locked away. His work, though, would lead to the death of millions and the end of knights.

1485 Battle of Bosworth Field, Britain
The last great charge of knights in armour ever seen in Britain.

KING RICHARD SITS ON TOP OF AMBIEN HILL NEAR BOSWORTH

HIS ENEMY HENRY TUDOR SITS AT THE BOTTOM. HIS CANNON AND ARROWS ANNOY RICHARD

RICHARD LEADS THE CHARGE DOWN THE HILL TO FINISH OFF HENRY

RICHARD IS KNOCKED OFF HIS HORSE AND HACKED TO DEATH BY HENRY'S FOOT SOLDIERS

RICHARD'S CROWN IS HANDED TO HENRY. RICHARD'S BODY IS STRIPPED AND THROWN OVER A HORSE TO BE CARTED OFF FOR A BURIAL

☠ **DID YOU KNOW…?** ☠

Only TWO Kings of England have died in battle: Harold at Hastings in 1066 and Richard III at Bosworth Field in 1485.

Harold started the battle in the best place – on the hill top. His enemy got Harold's army to charge down and get a battle battering.

Richard started the battle in the best place – on the hill top. His enemy got Richard's army to charge down and get a battle battering.

The lesson is?

> I SHOULD HAVE READ MY HORRIBLE HISTORIES BOOKS

So the Battle of Bosworth Field was the last great charge of knights in shining armour. But the IDEA of warriors on horses, riding madly into the jaws of death, lived on for hundreds of years. Even to…

1854 Charge of the Light Brigade, the Crimea

During the Crimean War, British horsemen are told to attack Russian cannon. The cannon come off best. The French general Pierre Bosquet watches it and says…

> *It is magnificent, but it isn't war. It is stupidity.*

3 If YOU are a king then you should never go into battle without a few *Horrible Histories* books in your saddle-bags. You can at least die laughing.

The Victorian poet Alfred Lord Tennyson thinks it IS magnificent and makes a famous poem out of it…

Their's not to reason why,
Their's but to do and die:
Into the valley of Death
Rode the six hundred.
Cannon to right of them,
Cannon to left of them,
Cannon behind them
Volleyed and thundered;
Stormed at with shot and shell,
While horse and hero fell,
They that had fought so well
Came through the jaws of Death,
Back from the mouth of Hell,
All that was left of them,
Left of six hundred.

But hang on, Alf Lord T ... you make it sound worse than it was. What do you mean, 'All that was left of them'?

Only 157 of the 673 Brits were killed but, thanks to you, it is remembered as a 'massacre'. You should have been at Adrianople in AD 378!

Around 20,800 men died horribly in the rest of the Crimean War. They are forgotten but the men on horses are remembered as heroes.

Meanwhile 16,300 other soldiers died of disease in the horrible hospitals where the floors were awash with sewage. They lay on straw beds while fleas and rats hopped over them. But 'Pee to the left of them, poo to the right of them!' doesn't make such a good poem, does it?

Knight work

The Persians probably had the first knights in armour. A Roman general, Ammianus Marcellinus, said...

All their men were covered in iron, and all parts of their bodies were covered with thick plates. They were made so that the stiff joints matched with those of their arms and legs. Metal masks were fitted to their faces. Their entire bodies were covered with metal so arrows that fell upon them could only hit through tiny openings in the eye, or where the tips of their noses let them breathe.

The Romans had been beaten by men in armour. Great leaders like Charlemagne and the warlords of Europe decided they needed soldiers on horses to fight the invaders on horses. But horses cost money. Peasants couldn't afford warhorses.

So the peasants continued to fight as foot soldiers (infantry) while posh people with money got themselves warhorses and rode into battle (cavalry)⁴.

These horse soldiers must have felt special because they were on horses while the common soldiers were on foot. Emperor Charlemagne (King of the Franks from AD 771 to 814) said to these horse soldiers...

---

4 How did a knight in armour get into his saddle? He climbed up with the help of a squire or a high block. Forget the stories about cranes hauling them up. There is nothing to prove that old tale is true. On a battlefield you couldn't have thousands of cranes carried along just so a knight could get going.

RIGHT LADS, YOU PAY A LOT OF MONEY FOR THOSE HORSES AND WEAPONS. IF YOU FIGHT FOR *ME* I'LL REWARD YOU BY GIVING YOU LOTS OF LAND AND SLAVES

IT'S A DEAL

Notice the slaves didn't have a lot of say in the matter! They were just handed over to their new lord – the knight.

So a knight was a soldier who fought on horseback (usually) and served a lord.

The Normans came along around AD 1000 and made the knight idea really work. The king gave his lords some land and they 'paid' for it by fighting for him in his wars.

By then the knight needed a lot more than a helmet and a horse. These new knights ALSO had to pay for:

1 WEAPONS – because swords don't grow on trees

2 ARMOUR – mail-to-measure costs more than mail-order

3 TENT – because you might rust solid if you sleep in the open

4 BAGGAGE HORSES – because taxis haven't been invented

5 FINE ROBES MADE OF TOP-QUALITY WOOL, SILK OR VELVET AND TRIMMED WITH FUR – because you can't cuddle a lady when you're wearing armour

6 FEASTS – for when the king comes calling

7 TRIPS TO THE ROYAL COURT – because most kings are so thick they need you to tell them what to do

8 CLOTHES FOR THE ORDINARY SOLDIERS – because they'd look pretty stupid rushing to battle quite bare

9 FOOD FOR THE ORDINARY SOLDIERS – because they'd only whinge if you starve them

And, most expensive of all:

10 A CASTLE – because you need a local criminal court, a place for collecting taxes and a place to shelter your peasants when their villages are attacked

❦ **DID YOU KNOW…?** ❦

Persian King Cyrus beat his enemy Croesus in 550 BC by putting his men on camel-back! The enemy horses were so scared they ran away and Cyrus won the battle.

Captured Croesus was tied to a stake, ready to be made into a sort of burger king, when he said…

King Cyrus thought it was a clever thing to say and that it was a shame to burn such a wise man. He had the flames put out and spared the life of Croesus. This being-kind-to-enemies stuff is what you expect of a knight … even a knight on camel-back.

Perfect Paladins

'Paladin' meant 'man of the palace'. It was the name Emperor Charlemagne gave to his 12 favourite knights. Paladins were the real knights in shining armour – even before shining armour had been invented.

They were the knights who rode out looking left and right for wrongs to right and baddies to fight.

One of the first great paladins was Roland who fought for Charlemagne in AD 778.

There is a famous poem that tells his tale.

'The Song of Roland' poem says Charlemagne is fighting the Saracens in Spain and goes off through a mountain pass to safety. He says to Roland…

But when the Saracens attack Roland finds he is short of men. All he has to do is blow his trumpet. His men tell him…

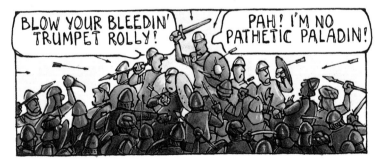

He is too proud, too stubborn. His men are massacred. THEN he blows his trumpet and prays for help...

Roland is the last to die. He tries to break his sword so it can't be taken as a trophy by the enemy. Then, just before he dies, he hears Charlemagne returning.

What a knightly nutcase. His men didn't have to die. Maybe he needs a NEW poem? Something like.

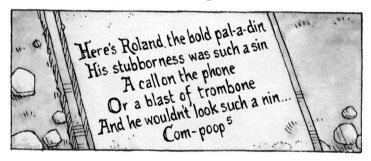

Roland really DID die in AD 778 but most of the poem is a big fib. Still lots of knights tried to copy the Roland in the story. If YOU want to be a knight you need to know it.

---

5 Yes, all right, the poem isn't perfect yet. We're working on it. If you think you can do better, smarty-pants, you should be writing a book not reading one.

Knight weapons

Yes, you know knights have swords and lances. Those lances may look like fun-fight sticks that knights used in jousts so no one was hurt. But they were dangerous toys.

In 1120 Usamah, a writer, told the story of a lance being driven through the back of a fully armoured Christian knight. It came out through his chest. The knight survived!

Then there are some REALLY nasty weapons.

Here are a few other things knights used. (Not the sort you see in school books – these are odd ones they don't tell you about in case you use them in the war against teachers!)

Maybe you can copy one or two…

SPIKED GAUNTLET… PUNCH THE ENEMY IN THE FACE WITH THIS AND HE'LL BE ABLE TO WHISTLE WITHOUT OPENING HIS MOUTH. GREAT THING IS YOUR ENEMY CAN DISARM YOU IN A FIGHT

SPEAR… AT FIRST KNIGHTS USED THEIR LANCES FOR THROWING AT ENEMIES – LIKE A SPEAR. PRACTISE THE JAVELIN IN YOUR PE LESSONS

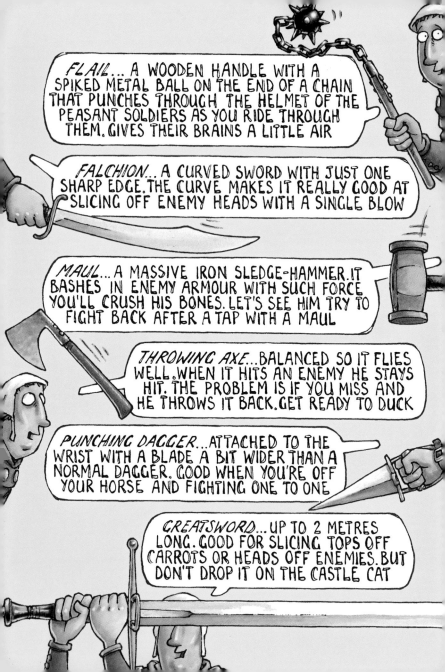

BEC-DE-CORBIN… A SORT OF PICK AXE THAT ALSO HAS A SPEAR POINT ON THE END. STAB OR JAB THROUGH THE ARMOUR. YOU COULD SAY… TAKE YOUR PICK! HA! HA!

MORNING STAR… A WOODEN POLE WITH A SPIKED IRON KNOB ON THE END. LIKE A FLAIL BUT EASIER TO CONTROL WHEN YOU ARE CLOSE UP TO AN ENEMY⁶

The nastiest weapon …

… was FEAR. Terrify your enemy and he won't be able to fight.

In the Crusades at Antioch (1098) both sides scalped or lopped off enemy heads … both the living and the dead.

They didn't just collect the heads as a trophy. The Christian knights lobbed 200 of them into the city and more of them were set up on stakes in view of the Muslim defenders to horrify them.

In reply, the Muslims killed any Christians still in the city and threw their heads over the walls.

A horrible form of head tennis.

6 A spiky ball on a stick doesn't SOUND very horrible – and morning star is SUCH a pretty name. But one knight in the Crusades was beaten so badly by the enemies' morning stars that a leg was torn from his body.

Castle curiosities

Lords in Norman times were nervous. They had just a few knights to keep those thousands of English peasants pleasant. If the English rebelled then there would be b-i-g trouble. So, just to be on the safe side the Normans built whacking great castles. The terrible towers gave a message to the pitiful peasants...

Don't even THINK about rebelling!

But they were NOT the most comfortable places to live. Cold and damp in winter, then in the summer they were … well, cold and damp. As for the toilets! You do NOT want to know about the toilets. You do? Oh, very well, read on. YOU asked for it…

Messy moats

A castle was often built with a band of water round the outside so attackers couldn't put ladders down. But all the toilets emptied into the moat and it soon began to fill up with human waste and smelled like a dead rat's gut. If you fell in you might not drown – but you would be poisoned if you swallowed any water.

FANCY A SWIM?

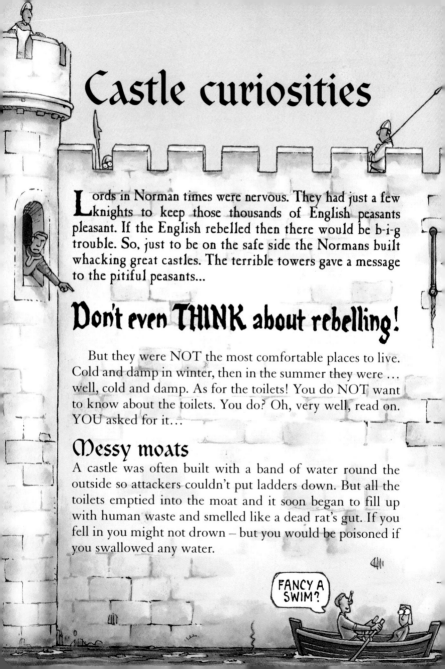

Fishy flavour

The moats were often filled with fish. The castle cooks would have the fish caught and serve them up for dinner. But would YOU want to feast on fish that fed on filth?

Gooey garderobes

The posh people in the castle had their own toilet rooms called garderobes – because that's where they guarded robes: kept their clothes. Why keep their best clothes in the toilet? Because moths like to lay their eggs in clothes and when the eggs hatch out with grubs they eat holes in the clothes. Hang your clothes in the toilet and the moths will keep away – they can't stand the smell.

Shmelly shafts

A toilet was often just a hole in the floor. Under the hole was a stone shaft that led down into the toilet pit below (or into the moat if you had one).

The trouble is, attackers could sometimes climb up this shaft and get into your castle. If you were REALLY unlucky you could be sitting on the toilet seat when they popped up!

WHO'S UNLUCKY?

Ashes to ashes

If you are at a feast you do NOT want to miss the tasty treats and the brilliant booze for a moment. So you would NOT want to say, 'Excuse me while I pop out to the little boys' (or girls') room!' and then wander down dark corridors looking for a loo, getting lost and cold and hungry. No, you would go to the fireplace in the dining hall and widdle in the ashes. Sizzle and hiss.

Putrid pits

Not every castle had a moat. Those castles without, had a toilet pit or 'cesspit' where all the poo collected. Of course it would begin to fill up. You needed someone to empty it with shovels, fill up wheelbarrows with it and cart it off. Would YOU like that wheely nice job? The men who did it were called 'gong farmers'. The waste could be spread over the fields to make the crops grow!

GOING
GOING
GONG

HORRIBLE HISTORIES HINT:
If you ever meet a gong farmer,
try not to shake hands with him.

Terrific toilets

If you were on guard duty, up on the castle walls, then you would not walk down for a midnight pee. You would just widdle over the wall.

HORRIBLE HISTORIES NOTE:
Do NOT do this if you are on guard duty at your school tournament – you will make a very good target for enemy arrows.

NOT THE CURTAINS!

Mopping-up job

Paper was expensive and hard to make in the Middle Ages. No one would use it for toilet paper. Instead you'd use a bit of straw or moss. Posh people might use a damp cloth. What did most knights use? Nothing.

Lousy leather

Often there were workshops inside the castle walls, including one for a 'tanner' – a man who took the skin of a cow and turned it into leather for jackets and shoes. He softened up the skin by putting it in a barrel with lots of juicy dog-poo and trampling it. Nice.

TOXIC TANNER

PONGY GONG FARMER

SPLISHY SPLOSHY

Bum job

The lords and knights of the castle didn't want to wander to the toilet shaft in the garderobe in the middle of the night. They used a potty set into a chair – known as a 'stool'. A servant would empty it in the morning. If you think THAT'S a bad job then you will feel sorry for the servant of monster knight, Henry VIII. The servant's job was to follow Henry to the toilet and wipe his fat backside.

✠ DID YOU KNOW…? ✠

Stairways in castle towers go up clockwise. Why? If someone is chasing you up a castle tower then it is easier for a right-handed swordsman to back up the stairs. A right-handed attacker would find it difficult to chase after him. BUT some castles, like Caerphilly in Wales, have a couple of stairways that go up anti-clockwise. If you find you are fighting to get into your own tower then you would choose one of those!

GOOD BOY

1. DON'T...

Rotten rules

The Norman knights decided it would be much more fun if they had 'rules' about fighting.

A knight was supposed to stick to rules that became known as 'chivalry'. You know the sort of thing...

1. Go to the church often
2. Choose his friends carefully
3. Be brave in battle
4. Always be ready for battle
5. Spend his money wisely
6. Not go hunting too often
7. Take revenge if he is insulted
8. Take revenge if his sister is insulted
9. Do brave deeds for his lady
10. Die for his lady

BET MY LADY WOULDN'T DIE FOR *ME*

A German book of the 1100s said…

> *A young knight should woo a noble woman. He should knock at her door until it opens. He talks with her by her fireside for she will want to talk away the sorrows of her heart.*

HORRIBLE HISTORIES NOTES:

1. Cuddling is allowed but it must be kept secret. Public cuddling is not on. If the woman is unmarried then her dad will get upset with you. If the woman is married then her husband will get upset with you.

2. A married woman is best. She probably only married some lord as part of a deal about her land. She will be bored and lonely.

3. Only ever flirt with noble women. A knight who falls in love with a peasant – even a high-class peasant who washes between her toes – is a disgrace. It is best if the woman is even more noble than the knight. Loving a queen is probably best of all … unless you get caught, of course.

❊❊❊ DID YOU KNOW…? ❊❊❊

A Norman knight swore to prove his love for a lady. She told him to go off and pick up all the stones on the beaches of Brittany. What did he do? He went to bed and sulked for two YEARS. Served him right, really. Never ask a lady, 'What can I do to win your love?' She may not WANT her love to be won so she sets an impossible task.

Knight school

You didn't learn how to be a warrior over-knight. Oh, no, it took up to 14 years or even more.

This is what you had to do…

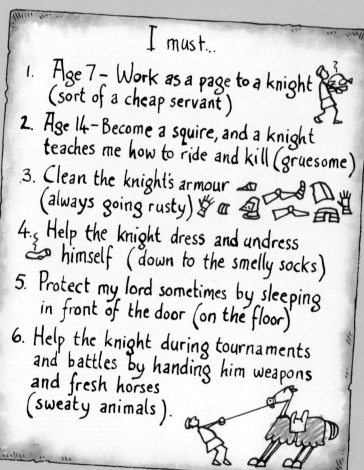

I must…

1. Age 7 – Work as a page to a knight (sort of a cheap servant)
2. Age 14 – Become a squire, and a knight teaches me how to ride and kill (gruesome)
3. Clean the knight's armour (always going rusty)
4. Help the knight dress and undress himself (down to the smelly socks)
5. Protect my lord sometimes by sleeping in front of the door (on the floor)
6. Help the knight during tournaments and battles by handing him weapons and fresh horses (sweaty animals).

7. Go with my master into battle and fight at his side (dangerous)
8. Bandage my lord's wounds (messy)
9. Sometimes move my knight away from the danger (heavy work)
10. Make sure he gets a good funeral (sad)

In the end you may have to die with your knight.

If you made it to 21 you could become a knight yourself. But first you'd have to have a bath.

That's bad – but Celtic knights in the Dark Ages bathed in a pot of horse-flesh soup. So it could be worse.

✦ DID YOU KNOW…? ✦

In 1306 Edward's son was to be knighted. To make it a special day another 300 young men were to be knighted at the same time.

Have you ever tried to get 300 men round one altar in a church? Don't. On that special day many were injured – two died.

As a squire you also learned good manners.

The manners were written down. Could you stick to these rules at YOUR school dinner table?

1. DO NOT clean your nails or your teeth with your eating knife[7].

2. DO NOT wipe your knife on the table cloth.

3. DO NOT play with the tablecloth or blow your nose on your napkin[8].

4. DO NOT dip your bread in your soup.

5. DO NOT fill your soup spoon too full or blow on your soup.

6. DO NOT eat noisily or clean your bowl by licking it out.

7. DO NOT speak while your mouth is full of food[9].

8. DO NOT spit over the table but spit on the floor.

9. DO NOT tear at meat but cut it with a knife first.

10. DO NOT take the best food for yourself[10]. Share it.

BET MY LADY WOULDN'T DINE WITH ME EITHER

7 Scratching your head at the table 'as if clawing at a flea' was also impolite.
8 But it was common for people to use their fingers to pick their nose at the table.
9 You could burp at the dining table ... but not TOO close to someone's face!
10 And you are asked not to steal food off someone else's plate.

Polite
punch-ups

Of course the knight fights had to have rules too and the French came up with these in the 1100s. They were called 'tournaments'.

These early tournaments were like little battles and known as 'mêlées'.

A sort of brutal game with rules – like netball.

Knights would split up into two teams with their lords as team captains. There could be 200 knights on each team.

The field of play would be several square miles and include fields, rivers and woods.

Mêlées took war and turned it into a game. The aim was to capture an opposing knight and hold him to ransom. There were no referees or judges at first but there were 'safe areas' where a battered knight would be allowed to escape and rest.

What do you imagine the rules were?

Pick the rules you would agree with…

1 Do not gang up in a group to attack a single knight.

2 Do not attack a knight who has lost some important armour.

3 Do not use bows, arrows or crossbows.

4 Do not hide and ambush opponents.

5 Do not touch a knight in a 'safe area'.

6 Do not attack a knight who has lost his horse.

7 Do not attack a knight from behind.

8 Do not attack a knight waving a white flag.

9 Do not strike below the belt with a sword.

10 Do not try to kill another knight.

Answer: The only rules you had to stick to were numbers 5 and 10. You could do 1, 2, 3, 4, 6, 7, 8 and 9.

In time the tournaments became one-on-one fights between knights with lances. This was called 'tilting' and it was very dangerous.

Henry II of France (1519–1559) went tilting against Gabriel de Montgomery.

Montgomery begged the King not to fight. King Henry insisted. The two men put on their helmets, mounted their horses and charged at one another with their lances. Montgomery's lance shattered and splinters went into Henry's face.

After ten days in agony the King died.

Top tournament tips

If mêlées had no rules then it was easy to cheat. Jousting involved two knights charging at one another with lances. These jousts had more rules but it was still possible to trick the referee and cheat to win.

Of course it was a huge disgrace to be caught cheating. Knights agreed it was better to lose with honour than to win with a trick. But you're not a knight and you can be a bit underhand if you want to. So, if you ever find yourself in a mêlée or a joust, then here are a few hints on how to succeed without actually cheating. Some villainous knights actually used these dodges …

1. Don't join in the mêlée at the start. Wait for the others to tire themselves out and then go in and grab a few exhausted knights. Philip of Flanders used this trick a lot … until someone tried the same trick on him and beat him!

2. When you are supposed to be fighting with blunted lances then take a sharp one into the fight. In 1290 Duke Ludwig of Bavaria died when a sharp lance pierced his throat armour. What a pain in the neck for Ludwig!

3. Have your armour made so you can be screwed on to your saddle! Knights who did this didn't fall off. Opposing knights got very angry at this trick though. In the 1300s it was banned. In the 1400s Lord Wells accused a knight of being screwed to his saddle. Lord Wells was wrong and had to grovel and say 'Sorry!'

4. Grab a wounded knight after the mêlée has finished and the knights are on their way back to dinner. William Marshal of England did this when a knight fell off his horse and broke a leg when riding home. Wily Willy captured him and demanded a ransom.

5. Have special armour made. A metal glove (gauntlet) that locks itself around a lance keeps it steady and it is easier to hit the target. Another rule was added to make this illegal - if you were caught.

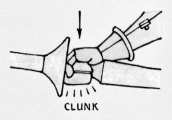

CLUNK

6. In a foot fight with axes, drop your axe and rush at your opponent. Then, as he raises his axe to strike, draw your dagger and stab him under the arm. In a 1408 tournament a knight tried this on his deadly enemy – this was not a fight for fun for them – but the king managed to stop him just in time. Others were not so lucky.

7. Use a lance that's longer and thicker than everyone else's! Bohemian knights did this in 1310 and they were unbeatable. Everyone refused to fight them ... so they fought each other instead!

8. In later tournaments you scored points by breaking your lance against your opponent's shield as you charged towards one another. The knight breaking the most lances was declared the winner. The trick is to have your lance made with a tip as frail as a glass butterfly and they'll break every time!

9. Catch your opponent asleep. In 1242 The Earl of Atholl knocked Walter Biset off his horse in a tournament. Walter waited till night fell when he crept into the Earl's tent and murdered him.

10. Have your opponent beaten up. A gang of squires with wooden clubs can jump on an opponent as he is on his way to the tournament. With a few broken ribs, legs and head he will not fight nearly so well.

Round tables

As tournaments became more organized they grew into events called 'Round Tables'. Everyone knows the story of King Arthur and his Round Table knights.

No one is quite sure who the real Arthur was – or if he ever really existed – but knights saw him as a good story to copy. So they...

• sat at a round table where everyone was equal. Before there had been a separate 'High' table for the king and his most powerful friends

• wandered around the world as 'knight errants' – looking for good causes to fight for and ladies to help

CARRYING YOUR SHOPPING WAS NOT QUITE WHAT I HAD IN MIND

• took part in tournaments dressed as King Arthur's knights (though King Arthur would never have jousted with lances)
• organised 'Round Table' events – the first was in Cyprus in 1223 – with jousting and other sports

If you want your own Round Table event then you could try some of the games the knights played. These included …

Casting the Stone

Competitors take it in turns to stand on a mark, pick up a large stone and throw it as far as they can.

The one who throws it furthest wins.

You may recognize this as the modern sport of shot put. And the groovy Greeks played this two thousand years before the knights, of course. (If you are too feeble to Cast The Stone then try something smaller and call it Putting the Pebble.)

Throwing the Lance

Competitors stand behind a mark. They pick up a lance and throw it.

The place the point lands is marked. The furthest throw is the winner.

Again, you'll recognize this as the modern sport of javelin. (If you are too much of a wimp to Throw the Lance then challenge your weedy friends to Propelling the Pencil.)

Cheerless churches

The Church thought it was fine to massacre millions of people who weren't Christian, but they didn't like tournaments where knights hurt one another for fun!

In 1130 a church law said:

> The church bans all of these detestable markets or fairs where knights meet to show off their strength and courage. At these meetings men are often killed and their souls are in danger of going to hell. If any man is killed at such a contest then be will not be allowed a church burial.

So there! Get yourself killed in a tournament and you won't be buried in a churchyard. But this didn't stop most knights. The truth is, they didn't expect to be killed so they weren't too worried about the church's threat!

King Richard I (the Lionheart) tried to get round the church's ban by selling tournament 'licences' in 1194. (He said the church would agree to his well organized punch-ups.) He created five official tournament fields in England.

Knights expected to end the day's jousting by having a bath, a rest and a cuddle from a beautiful lady. One priest called Thomas of Cantimpre warned that the knights would be disappointed. He told a story of what happened when one group of knights ignored a church request to stop fighting…

Hear what happened in the year of our Lord 1243 in Germany near the noble town of Neuss.

Many dukes, counts, barons and knights gathered for a tournament. Brother Bernard from the order of preachers arrived and begged them, almost in tears, not to hold this tournament. He asked them to go and fight for the Christian church in Hungary and Poland. The Count of Castris laughed at Brother Bernard and began the tournament.

Early in the morning a huge cloud appeared like a clod of earth with birds like crows hovering and croaking around it. These were devils who knew what was coming. When the tournament began the knights and their squires fell in such heaps that everyone knew this was the sport of the devil, not the sport of men. The total dead was 367 and one of the first to die was the Count of Castris.

So, be warned you knights. The Devil is waiting in Hell for those who fight in these evil tournaments. He has a suit of armour waiting for you and it is covered with spikes on the inside. He has a bath waiting for you – a bath of flames, a bed for your rest – a bed of red-hot iron, and the love of a lady fair - who is a huge and horrible toad. Even if you survive then the ghosts of those who die will return to haunt your dreams every night.

The truth is that 42 men died at Neuss, not Thomas's 367. He was wrong about that. So maybe he was also wrong about the red-hot iron bed and the cuddly toad.

The church eventually gave up trying to stop knights from having their sport.

Arthur's knights

Some of the most famous knights probably never existed. King Arthur may have been a British warrior in the 500s, long before knights in shining armour were around. But hundreds of years later stories were invented about him, about the knights of his Round Table and about his enemies.

Here they are with their horrible tales...

King Arthur

His story: The warrior king of Britain. He gathers 1,600 knights to defend the kingdom and they all sit around the same round table. Sixteen HUNDRED! What a table. Imagine asking someone at the far side to pass the salt[11].

But there are all sorts of problems with these 1,600 blokes sharing a table. For a start, that Lancelot chats up Arthur's wife, Guinevere, and that causes all sorts of bother.

11 If every knight had a metre of table then the bloke across the other side would be 500 metres away. By the time he passed the salt your dinner would be cold!

End of the knight: Arthur gets into a war with the evil knight Mordred and they meet to make a deal.

Arthur says...

WE ARE HERE TO MAKE PEACE. IF ANYONE DRAWS A SWORD THEN WE FIGHT

As luck would have it a poisonous snake runs over the battlefield. A knight draws his sword to kill the snake. Oooops!

It's a fight to the death – Arthur's death.

But is he REALLY dead? Or just sleeping?

And if he's sleeping does he have an alarm clock?

Sir Lancelot of the Lake

His story: Baby Lancelot is stolen by the Lady of the Lake and brought up under water. (He grows up a bit wet.)

While travelling, he is challenged by Sir Turquine, one of the enemies of the Round Table knights[12]. Lancelot slays him and then goes on to free Castle Tintagel from giants.

He always wins at tournaments … but when he starts flirting with King Arthur's wife he is finished. (She is burned to death as a punishment so she is even more finished.)

At least he saves his daughter, Elaine, from a tub of boiling water where she had been imprisoned for years.

12 Some people say this enemy group lived in a deep, dark forest that is now the city of Manchester!

End of the knight: Rather nice end, really. He goes off to be a hermit and spends his life praying. He probably dies quietly.

Sir Galahad

His story: He is Lancelot's son and the perfect knight. He sets off to look for the Holy Grail – the magical cup that Jesus drank from and then dripped blood into as he hung on the cross.

The poets said Galahad had 'the strength of ten'. (But they don't say ten what. Ten tomatoes?)

He finds the Holy Grail at the court of King Pelles in the Castle of Corbenic. And would you believe it? King Pelles is his grandad!

End of the knight: He finds the Holy Grail and you can't top that. He dies. There is nothing much else for him to do really.

Sir Gawain

His story: At a New Year party a strange Green Knight arrives with a challenge.

> ONE MAN MAY STRIKE ME ONE BLOW WITH AN AXE. IF I SURVIVE I WILL RETURN IN A YEAR. THEN I WILL HAVE ONE STRIKE AT HIM

Gawain knocks the Green Knight's head off, but the stranger picks up his head and promises to be back next year. Gawain meets the Green Knight's wife by chance. He is so nice to her the Green Knight lets Gawain off with a nick to the neck.

Gawain goes off and kills his own dad, Pellinore. (Maybe he didn't give him his pocket money.)

End of the knight: Who knows?

Sir Agravaine

His story: This little sneak decides to catch Lancelot and Guinevere having a cuddle. He dashes into the room and sort of says, 'Aha! I've caught you at it!'

End of the knight: Lancelot picks up his sword and chops Agravaine to death. Let that be a lesson to us all.

> MY HERO

Mordred

His story: He is the son of Arthur's sister – so he has to be nice to Uncle Arthur, doesn't he?

No. He pinches the throne while Arthur is away fighting.

Angry Arthur returns. Lancelot defeats Mordred in battle, but Mordred survives.

End of the knight: He is locked away with the corpse of Queen Guinevere and left to starve. First he eats her corpse but starves in the end anyway[13].

Horrible Histories note:

Parents are always telling you 'Eat your green bits, they'll do you good'. Tell them, 'Mordred tried eating his queen bits – but it didn't do him any good at all'.

Mind you her eyes must have tasted nice. I mean, we all like jelly 'n' ice cream.

13 Of course Guinevere was BURNED to death, so it's not as if he was eating her raw, is it? She may have been a bit overcooked but it's better than eating uncooked meat.

Sir Geraint

His story: Sir Geraint helps an old knight, Sir Yniol, to get back his lands. Geraint falls in love with Sir Yniol's daughter, Enid.

But then he hears her complaining that he is a lazy knight and he is sure she has another boyfriend. He is so jealous he makes her prove how much she loves him. But for a while he is really, really mean and won't let her even speak! He then goes off and does brave deeds to show his love for her. They fall in love all over again. So sweet it makes you a little bit sick.

End of the knight: No sticky end (no sticky Enid either). They live happily ever after.

Sir Tristan

His story: He goes off to Ireland to bring Isolde back for her wedding to Mark – his uncle, the King of Cornwall. But Tristan and Isolde drink a magic drink and fall madly in love. Isolde marries Mark anyway – then he finds out she is really in love with Tristan. Uh-ohh!

End of the knight: Mark kills Tristan, as you do. Isolde goes off and dies of a broken heart … as you also do.

Sir Balin

His story: He is so-o-o unlucky. He finds a lady who has been forced to wear a sword and sets her free of it. He is warned...

IF YOU KEEP THE SWORD YOU WILL KILL THE PERSON YOU LOVE MOST IN THE WORLD

What would YOU do if you found a sword with a curse? Drop the sword down the nearest toilet? Yes.

What does batty Balin do? He keeps it. He is known as 'The Knight with Two Swords'. Then he meets a man in battle...

End of the knight: Balin kills the other knight in battle, but is badly wounded himself. Before he dies he takes off his enemy's helmet.

Who is it?

Why, it's his lovely brother Balan! Oh, no, the curse has come true. Balin drops down dead from his wounds.

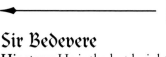

Sir Bedevere

His story: He is the last knight left standing at the end of Arthur's last battle against Mordred. Arthur says…

DO ME A FAVOUR, BEDEVERE. CHUCK ME OLD SWORD EXCALIBUR BACK IN THE LAKE – THEN COME BACK HERE AND TELL ME WHAT YOU SAW

Now Bed is a little bad. 'Shame to throw away that nice sword when scrap metal prices are so high!' So he hides the sword and tells Arthur, 'It sank'.

Arthur sends Bedevere back to do it again. When he REALLY throws it in the lake a lady's hand rises from the water and pulls it under.

Arthur can die in peace – and in pieces, of course.

End of the knight: Like Lancelot, Bedevere goes off to be a hermit and dies of old age. Sounds about right: Sir Bed dies in bed.

Dressed to kill

If you wanted to be a knight you had to dress to kill. But our terrific Horrible Histories researchers came across this knight who was dressed to be killed. We managed to make this sketch before the man-in-a-can started to go mouldy.

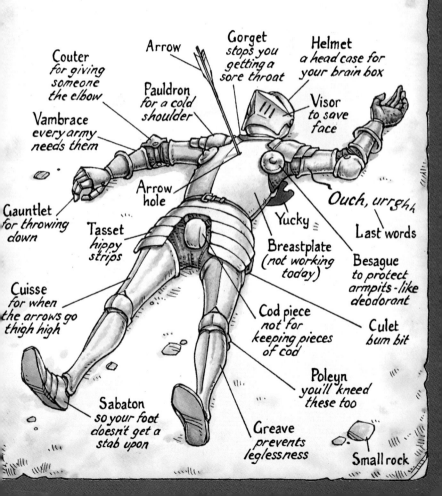

Couter
for giving someone the elbow

Arrow

Gorget
stops you getting a sore throat

Helmet
a head case for your brain box

Pauldron
for a cold shoulder

Visor
to save face

Vambrace
every army needs them

Arrow hole

Gauntlet
for throwing down

Tasset
hippy strips

Yucky

Ouch, urrghh
Last words

Breastplate
(not working today)

Besague
to protect armpits - like deodorant

Cuisse
for when the arrows go thigh high

Cod piece
not for keeping pieces of cod

Culet
bum bit

Poleyn
you'll kneed these too

Sabaton
so your foot doesn't get a stab upon

Greave
prevents leglessness

Small rock

Cruel crusades

The Christian knights of Europe set off to conquer the 'Holy Land' that was ruled by the Muslims. They called their wars 'The Crusades'.

They were supposed to be fighting with God on their side. But God must have been upset at some of the bloody and bizarre things that happened...

1 The most vicious victory for the Christians came at Jerusalem in 1099. A writer said:

The crusaders, excited by such a great victory, rushed through the streets and into the houses and mosques killing all that they met, men, women and children alike. All that afternoon and all through the night the massacre went on. When Raymond of Aguilers went to visit the temple the next morning he had to pick his way through corpses and blood that reached up to his knees.

2 At the Battle of Cerami in 1063 the spirit of St George was said to have turned up to help when 130 Normans defeated thousands of Muslims. The soldiers reported…

SAINT GEORGE APPEARED ON A WHITE HORSE WITH A LANCE. THERE WAS A FLAG ON THE END OF THE LANCE WITH A WONDERFUL CROSS ON IT. WE'D HAVE LOST IF HE HADN'T LED OUR CHARGES

The Pope believed the story and sent a flag, like the one in the vision, for the Christians to carry into future battles.

St George turned up again 35 years later at the battle for Antioch in the Holy Land. An unknown writer said…

Our soldiers saw a countless army of men on white horses whose banners were all white. When our men saw this they realized this was help sent by Christ and the leader was St George. This is quite true for many of our men saw it.

But sadly old Georgie wasn't around at Hattin in 1187 when the Crusaders were smashed. Perhaps it was his day off!

3 In 1065, when the First Crusade set off, one group of pilgrims found a goose that they thought was sent by God. They began to play 'Follow My Leader' with it and the goose led them to the Holy Land. (When they ran out of food they probably played 'Eat My Leader'.)

4 On 15 April 1291 a group of Templar knights sneaked into a Turkish camp on foot. One knight tripped over a tent rope and fell head first into a ditch that the Turks used as a toilet.

He drowned in the sewage. Yeuch!

The rest of the force were captured and executed.

Their heads were tied round the neck of a horse and presented to the Sultan next day.

5 The Christians had won great victories in Europe where their charging knights smashed the enemy to the ground. But when the Crusaders met the Muslim forces they had problems. The Muslims didn't line up and wait to be smashed to the ground! Instead they rode in a circle around the Crusaders and shot arrows at them from a distance. Many Norman knights believed there was a reason for this:

Other knights just thought the Muslims must be cowards. After some bitter batterings the Christians learned to respect their Muslim enemies.

6 At Hosn al Akrad in the Holy Land in 1099 the Crusaders were ready to attack. They needed to get into the city before they starved.

The defenders knew they would be massacred the next day.

So the evening before the attack they set free a few hundred sheep, who ran for their pastures in the hills. The hungry attackers ran after them and the defenders managed to sneak out.

Next day the Crusaders attacked and wondered why the Turks didn't fight back! Would ewe believe it? The place was empty.

7 In 1272 the English King Edward I was in Palestine. A visitor arrived and said he had to speak to the King. They showed him into Edward's tent. 'Your Majesty,' the man said, 'my business is so secret I must speak to you alone!' Edward sent his guards away. As soon as they were alone the man drew a poisoned knife and stabbed Ed in the arm. Ed kicked at the killer, knocked him down with a stool and grabbed at the knife.

In the struggle the King received another wound on the forehead. The man was overpowered but Ed was seriously ill. He even made his will. But his luck held and he survived. One poem says:

> **Eleanor his gentle wife—**
> **Sucked out his wound and saved his life**

Another story says she made such a fuss the doctor sent her from the room and cured the King without her help. That's more likely.

8 At Acre in 1191 Richard the Lionheart was desperate to drive out the enemy. He tried one of the oddest weapons in history ever! He used catapults to lob 100 beehives over the walls.

There were eight Crusades lasting almost 200 years. The Christians won a few battles and captured a few towns but, in the end, they left the Holy Land defeated.

DID YOU KNOW…?

Crusaders faced a dreadful weapon in the Middle East: 'Greek Fire'. It caught alight as soon as it touched sea water and threatened their ships. But the Normans believed that throwing sand over the Greek Fire or pouring pee on it was the best way to kill the flames. That is not to say they stood there and risked singeing their piddling bits. If they expected an attack of Greek Fire they'd collect barrels of the stuff.

The recipe for Greek Fire has been lost since it was used in the Middle Ages so we can't test the fire-fighting methods to see if they're true.

Warrior women

Knights were supposed to look after women, fight for them and care for them. But women in the Middle Ages sometimes came along to the fights.

Women went on Crusades along with the men. The Second Crusade had women riding with the men and sitting astride their horses. The historian who wrote about this was quite shocked at the idea!

Women Crusaders helped in emergencies to defend the cities they had captured. One historian tells of a woman who was helping to build an earth wall when she was struck by a Turk's javelin. As she died she begged…

BURY ME IN THE WALL SO MY CORPSE CAN BECOME PART OF THE DEFENCES

Crusaders often took old women with them and these women had two main jobs. One was to wash the Crusaders' clothes and the other was to comb their hair and keep their heads free of lice. One writer said…

These women are better than monkeys.

Women on the Crusades were expected to find food and cook it. That was hard in times of famine. In 1191 at the siege of Acre the cooks used:

Shopping list

+ Leaves and tree bark
+ Soup from animal skins
+ Grains of wheat found in animal droppings
+ Bones that have been chewed by dogs
+ Slices taken from enemy dead
  – the bum is the best they say

Waiting widows

A woman whose husband went missing on a Crusade didn't always know if he was dead or alive. If he was dead she could marry again. If no one knew what had happened then lawyers could set a time limit.

Some courts said a woman could marry if her husband had been missing five years. But one said:

YOU MAY MARRY AGAIN WHEN HE HAS BEEN GONE ONE HUNDRED YEARS!

GOSH THANKS

Fearless females

Not all women were homely housewives. Some women in the Middle Ages were as fearless as the men. In the Third Crusade many women took part in the siege of Acre. They attacked the Turks with huge knives and brought Turkish heads, dripping with blood, back to their homes.

Here are some of the most famous fearless females of the Middle Ages:

Jeanne de Clisson

In 1313 Olivier de Clisson was executed on the orders of Philip the Fair, King of France. His wife, Jeanne, decided he was Philip the Un-fair and decided to get her own back.

First she sold off all of her lands to raise money. Then she bought three warships; they were painted black and had red sails. Admiral Jeanne began destroying Philip's ships and murdering their crews ... but she always left two or three alive to carry the story back to the King.

She liked to chop off enemy heads herself.

Madame de Montfort

In 1341 Madame de Montfort was left to defend the town of Hennebont in Brittany when her husband was taken prisoner. She rode out in full armour to lead her soldiers. She told the women of Hennebont to cut their skirts short; that way they could run up to the ramparts with stones and pots of boiling tar to pour over the attackers.

When the attackers grew tired, Madame de Montfort led a group of knights out of the town through a secret gate. They rode round behind the enemy and destroyed half of the army. Hennebont was saved.

When her husband died Madame de Montfort carried on the war. But she went mad, was captured by the English and locked away for 30 years until she died.

Lady Mabel of Belleme

Mabel plotted to poison her husband's enemy, Arnold of Echauffour, who was visiting them.

She placed a poisoned goblet of wine on the table and waited. Sadly her brother-in-law, Gilbert, came in sweaty and hot from hunting. He cried…

… snatched up the poison cup and swallowed the lot.

He died. Now, if you'd been Mabel, you'd have given up, wouldn't you? Not her. She bribed one of Enemy Arnold's servants to put poison in his food, which he did. Arnold died. Second time lucky!

The Countess of Buchan

The Countess of Buchan defended Berwick Castle against Edward I. He was so furious he forgot that a knight was supposed to give women respect. When he finally took the castle he hung her over the battlements in an iron cage.

Joan of Arc (Jeanne d'Arc)

The most famous woman knight of all was a French farmer's daughter … Jeanne.

Jeanne heard angels' voices telling her to lead the French soldiers to victory against the invading English. Against all the odds this is what she did.

In spite of being wounded with a crossbow bolt she defeated the English at the siege of Orléans in 1429. Unfortunately she couldn't defeat France's other enemy, Burgundy. The Burgundians captured Jeanne and very sensibly sold her to the English. The English couldn't execute her as a soldier, so they said she was a witch and burned her at the stake. Jeanne's big crime? Wearing men's clothes!

WELL HAVE YOU TRIED TO FIND ARMOUR IN A SIZE 8?

Terrible Templars

In 1118, when the Crusades were splattering blood all over Palestine, Hugh de Payens said, 'Let's have some SPECIAL knights. Knights who can guard Christians on their trip through the Holy land.'

'Great idea!' a few other knights said.

Hugh added, 'Just the posh lads, of course.'

'Goes without saying,' they agreed.

'We'll set up near the Temple of Solomon in Jerusalem. We'll call ourselves Order of the Temple, the Knights of the Temple of Solomon in Jerusalem!' Hugh told them.

'Ooooh! Bit of a mouthful that.'

'Righty-ho … let's call them Templars for short.'

'Terrific!' they cheered.

'No. Templars,' Hugh said.

And so the Templars began.

The Templars promised to live a simple life and stay poor – their sign was two men on one horse…

THIS IS A SIGN THAT WE ARE SO POOR WE DON'T EVEN HAVE A HORSE EACH

AND IT IS A SIGN OF THE WAY WE HELP ONE ANOTHER

I THINK IT'S A SIGN OF CRUELTY TO HORSES

But these 'poor' knights managed to collect a fortune! They became moneylenders. And where there's money there's trouble – jealousy and greed are terrible things.

Massacring monks

The Templars were warrior monks. They had NOTHING to do with women and ate very little. Some of them almost starved themselves to death to prove how much they loved their God. So a rule said they had to eat in pairs – so one could make sure the other ate properly.

You could always spot a Templar in battle because he wore the Templar cross on his tunic. It looks like this…

But they were NOT the first knights to think of the *Horrible Histories* ancient joke…

Templar trouble

The Templars were supposed to fight their Muslim enemies. But they spent a lot of time fighting their friends! A group of knights called the Hospitallers were the Templars' great rivals. Stories began to spread about the Templars.

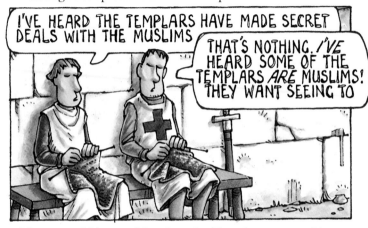

There would be trouble when the Templars returned home to France.

☠ DID YOU KNOW...? ☠

A group of German Knights Templar, the Livonian Brothers, fought in northern Europe, around the Baltic Sea. The knights would cut and burn their way through pagan lands leaving nothing living and the land a waste. The natives of Livonia hated the knights so bitterly that they would skin them alive and offer them as sacrifices to their gods. The knights were there looking to conquer the whole country and make it their own special Hospitallers' land. It was a Crusade of the north and was as bitter and cruel as the Crusades in Palestine.

Phoul Philip

Philip IV the Fair (1268–1314) was King of France. He did a bad job of running the country and the peasants were starving and after his blood. He came up with a vicious way to raise money – and save his skin. He accused the Knights Templar of worshipping the devil. He said they did disgusting things like piddling on the crosses in church.

Philip wanted the Templars to own up to their crimes. On 13 October 1307 he had them all arrested. Most were tortured...

* There were no toilets in the cells and the knights were stripped naked and nearly starved in the process.

* One Templar had his feet oiled then set on fire, burning his feet until even the bones fell off. He was then given the blackened bones to carry to his trial.

* Others had their stomachs cut open and their guts burned while they were alive and watching this being done.

* Some Templars were beheaded and cut into pieces.

* Their arms and legs were pulled from their sockets.

* Their bones were broken by the twisting of bolts.

* Their lips were cut off and tongues cut out.

* They were forced to drink water from the moat which was filled with sewage from the toilets.

* Thirty-six men died in the first few days, others went mad and others suffered still more torture.

After the torture, 56 Templars were burned at the stake at the same time. The chief Templar (the Grand Master) was one of the victims. Philip was able to steal the Templars' money and buy his way out of trouble.

Pope Clement had agreed to the execution[14]. As the flames leapt up the Grand Master cried to Philip:

I shall meet you and Clement by God's seat before a year is past. You and your family, for thirteen generations, will be cursed!

Pope Clement died the next month ... King Philip died within seven months, though he was a healthy 46-year-old. Spooky or what?

14 Pope Clement would agree to anything Philip the Fair did. After all, Philip had the last Pope murdered and made sure his friend Clement got the job.

Knasty knights

Fighting was a rough and dirty job. In the early days knights would play little games like raiding an enemy village and tossing babies on the points of their spears.

Knights were well paid by their peasants – the peasants gave their lords two weeks' free work on his land every year as well as corn and meat for his table. They had to take turns guarding his castle and serving at his feasts.

In one French village, the peasants had to kiss the door of the knight's house. In another they had to stay up all night beating the village pond to stop the frogs from croaking and waking up the lord.

Some knights robbed their own villages and tortured the peasants. A French knight tortured peasants like this…

① FIRST I HALF-FILL A BOX WITH NAILS AND STONES…

② THEN I PLACE A PEASANT IN THE BOX…

③ THEN I CLOSE THE LID

SPLAT!

You could not be Mr Nice Guy all the time. But some knights seemed to enjoy being Mr Nasty Guy more than others. Here are some of their savage stories...

Bernard de Cahuzac, french knight, 1200s

Bernard cut off the hands and feet of 150 monks and nuns after an argument with the local abbot. Mad bad Bernie SAID they'd hidden their treasure from him and he wanted it. He then ripped out their eyes and left them to die.

LOOK ON THE BRIGHT SIDE—AT LEAST IT'S THE LAST WE'LL SEE OF HIM

I HOPE I DIE BEFORE THE NEXT JOKE

Bernard's wife joined in the fun. She enjoyed pulling out the nails of peasant girls and carving their bodies open.

William the Conqueror, King of England 1027–87

William marched on the town of Alençon. The defenders barred its gates. They had heard William was the grandson of a leather-worker (a tanner). So they hung leather skins over the walls and jeered...

Leather! Leather for the leather-worker's grandson!

William was furious. When he eventually captured the town he took 32 of the leading citizens of Alençon and paraded them in front of the townsfolk. Then he had their hands and feet cut off.

Godfrey of Bouillon, French knight, c. 1060-1100

At the Battle of Antioch Crusader Godfrey was challenged to a duel by a Turkish knight. They rode at each other and Godfrey used his huge sword to chop through the Turk's waist.

The top half of the Turk 'lay panting on the ground' while the bottom half went off at full speed on the horse!

Another Turk was cut by one of Godfrey's downward swipes; the sword went through his head, through his body, through the saddle and into his horse.

At the siege of Jerusalem he was the first to drive through the walls. He was sweating terribly with the effort but instead of having a drink of water he swallowed huge amounts of wine. It brought on a fever that killed him.

It's true what they say. Don't drink and drive.

Charles of Navarre, 1358

Charles of Navarre faced a peasant revolt led by William Cale. Charles invited Cale to talk peace. When Cale arrived Charles beheaded him, which is cheating.

HE WAS ONCE HEAD OF THE REVOLT. NOW HE'S JUST A REVOLTING HEAD

One story says Charles crowned Caen the 'King of the Peasants' before he beheaded him ... but he used a crown of red hot iron. Sizzle!

Mind you, William Cale's men HAD roasted a knight alive over an open fire, then made his wife and family eat the flesh. Don't feel TOO sorry for Cale the clot.

💀 DID YOU KNOW...? 💀

Charles of Navarre used a bandit chief to do his dirty work. How did Charles get out of paying the bandit? He invited the bandit leader to a feast and poisoned him.

Richard the Lionheart, King of England, 1100s

One historian said that Richard always kept a supply of prisoners with his army. Then, if his soldiers ran out of food, they could always eat the prisoners.

Saracen   Turk   Breakfast

That story may not be true. But it IS true that he took a lot of prisoners at the siege of Acre in 1191 during the Third Crusade – then gave the order to slaughter them all.

Philip Augustus, King of France, 1179–1223

Philip was supposed to be one of the 'good' knights but even he had his nasty moments.

In the war between England and France, King Richard I had French prisoners thrown off a cliff into the river to drown in their armour. He then took 15 French knights and cut out the eyes of 14 of them. Number 15 was left with one eye and his job was to lead the others back to their leader, Philip Augustus.

Philip was so furious he took 15 English knights and sent them back to Richard in the same way.

And when his dinner was badly cooked he had the cook tortured to death – slowly.

SLICE OFF ANY UNWANTED PIECES AND SEPARATE THE JOINTS. CHOP ROUGHLY THEN SOAK IN OIL. FINALLY ROAST OVER A MODERATE FLAME TILL BLACK AND CRISPY

Baldwin of Bouillon, French knight, 1058–1118

Crusader Baldwin became the first Christian King of Jerusalem. He led a group of 200 knights in an attack against a Muslim army ... then found there were 20,000 of the enemy surrounding him!

Most of his knights died, but Baldwin managed to get the fastest horse in town and galloped to safety in the hills.

At another Crusade battle he was left with just three other knights. They decided that it would be wise to hide in a bed of reeds. The Turks didn't bother to go into the reed bed after him ... they just set fire to the reeds. In fact the smoke screen helped him to escape, but he was badly burned.

Richard de Clare (known as 'Strongbow'), Earl of Pembroke, c. 1130–76

Strongbow was a Norman knight who invaded Ireland.

In May 1170 he attacked Waterford and the Irish defenders rode out to attack his army. The Irish were beaten and 70 of their men captured.

Strongbow could have held them prisoner or killed them quickly. He didn't.

First he took them to a cliff top and had their arms and legs broken. Then they were thrown into the sea.

There is a story that Strongbow discovered his son had acted like a coward. He took his sword and with one blow chopped his son in half at the waist.

Robert Guiscard, Norman knight 1015–85

A writer described this fierce Norman fighter…

Guiscard rode back into battle, spurred on by his rage. Burning with anger he cut off their hands and their feet. Here he would split a head open and the body with it. Sometimes he would rip open a belly and a chest – sometimes a man's ribs would be stabbed after cutting off his head.

NOT ONE OF LIFE'S GENTLE FLOWERS THEN

And one odd knight...

Ulrich of Liechtenstein, Bavarian knight, 1200s

Ulrich fell in love with his lady (he says) when he was just twelve years old. He then travelled round Europe as a knight-errant and proved his love by fighting anyone. On his tour (which he called the 'Venus Tour') he offered a gold ring to anyone who could defeat him. Ulrich claimed he had broken 307 lances. He dressed in a long blond wig and a woman's dress. (We don't know about his knickers.)

Awful orders

Knights always wanted to be part of a 'special' group – a bit like prefects at school. So they gave themselves special names like 'The Noble Order of the Yellow Cuckoo'[15] or titles – like 'Sir' or 'Baron' or 'Dad'.

Here are some of the orders you might like to join...

The Order of the Garter – founded 1387, England

These days the ruler of the United Kingdom can still make someone a knight in a very special club – the 'Order of the Garter'.

In the Middle Ages ladies tied ribbons round their legs to keep their stockings up. Elastic hadn't been invented, of course. In 1344 King Edward III decided to hold a Round Table Tournament at Windsor and make an 'Order of the Round Table'.

Then something happened to change his mind. This is the story...

IN 1347 EDWARD III WENT TO A FEAST AT CALAIS...

I FANCY A BIT OF A DANCE. MAY I HAVE THE PLEASURE, COUNTESS?

OOOOH, YOU ARE CHEEKY. GO ON THEN!

15 All right, I just invented that one for myself. I am chief cuckoo and get to wear the holy cuckoo nest on my head. If you want to join the Order of the Cuckoo then you must go for one whole hour saying nothing but 'Cuckoo'.

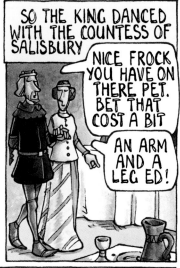

SO THE KING DANCED WITH THE COUNTESS OF SALISBURY

NICE FROCK YOU HAVE ON THERE PET. BET THAT COST A BIT

AN ARM AND A LEG ED!

WHEN SUDDENLY AN ACCIDENT HAPPENED...

GAWD! ME GARTER'S GONE

I NEVER TOUCHED IT!

THE SILK GARTER DROPPED TO THE FLOOR

TEE-HEE!

HOW SHOCKING

SHE'S GONE RED AS A BEETROOT

EDWARD WAS DISGUSTED BY THE WAY THE KNIGHTS AND LADIES BEHAVED

SHAME ON YOU. SHAME ON THOSE WHO THINK THIS IS SHAMEFUL

And that's the way it's stayed till this day. The members of the Order of the Garter have the words 'Shame on those who think this is shameful' on their badge – except it is written in French: *Honi soit qui mal y pense*.

But is the story true?

Some say the 'garter' was a strap that held armour together – the Order of the Garter had this strap sign to show how the knights were all 'held together'.

That stocking-garter story was just made up to poke fun at the order.

Horrible historians wouldn't do a thing like that. We simply ask…

WHAT WOULD HAVE HAPPENED IF THE LADY'S PANTS HAD FALLEN DOWN? WOULD WE HAVE THE 'ORDER OF THE KNICKERS'?

Well … no, actually, because in the days of Edward III people didn't wear any knickers.

Is the story true? Who knows. It's a history mystery.

🕱 DID YOU KNOW…? 🕱

If the British ruler wants a foreign king to be one of the 'Knights of the Garter' then they can't. Tough luck.

So they invented 'Stranger Knights' – foreign rulers who are friends of the 'Order of the Garter'.

The Order of the Golden Fleece – founded 1429, France

A French copycat called Philip the Good didn't want a Garter so he founded his own order – the Order of the Golden Fleece.

There is no story of him dancing with a golden sheep so the Order of the Golden Fleece is pretty boring ... unless you would care to make up a story? The members get to wear a golden sheep around their neck. (No, a model sheep, not a dead ram, you dummy.)

SORRY

The Order of the Bath – founded between 1399 and 1413, England

This British order was almost forgotten until George I dusted it off in 1725. But it was a much older idea.

Before a knight was knighted he had to have a bath.

I DON'T LIKE MY KNIGHTS TO FIGHT DIRTY

The order's motto is *Tria juncta in uno*, which as you know means 'Three in One'. Three what in one? Three men in the bath? Must be a pretty big bath! And in 1970 Queen Elizabeth II allowed women in the order.

She must believe in mixed bathing. Would you want to get in the water after two people had been in it?

The Order of the Thistle – founded 1687, Scotland

The Scottish 'Order of the Thistle' is for 16 people and the Royal Family. James VII of Scotland (who was also James II of England) founded the new order in 1687, but there may have been a much older one originally.

They have a nice Latin motto suitable for teachers, football hooligans and rottweiler dogs: *Nemo me impune lacessit*. Of course you don't need me to tell you what that means.

You do? Oh, all right. It means...

NO ONE HURTS ME AND GETS AWAY WITH IT

The Order of the Elephant – founded 1492, Denmark

How would you explain the Danish Knights having the 'Order of the Elephant'? Maybe this is for people who never forget! Maybe it's for people with a thick skin. Or maybe it's for people who spend the weekend tearing down trees with their nose. Luckily they don't have to wear an elephant round the neck.

The Most Illustrious Order of Saint Patrick – founded 1783, Ireland

George III invented this order for the Irish people in Britain. But in 1922 the south of Ireland split from Britain and it was never used again.

The order of St Patrick had a motto…

The jewels of the Knights of St Patrick were known as the Irish Crown Jewels. In 1907 they were pinched and no one has seen them since.

Sort of St Pat-nicked.

The Most Exalted Order of the Star of India – founded 1861, British Empire
Invented by Queen Victoria for top Indian people. They got to call themselves 'Knight Grand Commander'. A bit like the St Patrick Order, it vanished when the Empire vanished.

There are also some very odd orders:
Order of Motherhood – (date unknown), Albania
Given to women who have ten or more children. (To get the 'Order of the Syrian Family' you need to have SIXTEEN children.)

Order of Albert the Bear – founded 1870, Anhalt, Germany
Given to knights in the war against France. Bert the bear must have been pretty pleased as his knights rode out … probably bear back.

Order of the Ladies of the Hatchet – founded 1149, Barcelona
Given to ladies who helped defend the town of Tortosa when it was attacked by the Moors. They probably hatchet a plot.

Order of the Five Volcanoes – founded 1961, Guatemala
Given to people who have helped to unite Central America.

YOUR DAD'S GOT THE ORDER OF THE FIVE VOLCANOES?

YEAH, COS HE'S ALWAYS BLOWING HIS TOP

Order of the Book of Nature – founded 1945, Taiwan
Not knights of the wild-flower collection, but pilots who fought in the air to defend Taiwan.

Order of the Blood – founded 1839, Taiwan
Given by Tunisia to foreign rulers – no buckets of free blood, just a knighthood and a medal. Bleeding shame.

Order of the Prefect – founded 1946, Grott Street Primary School, Duckpool
Given to pupils who suck up to teachers, take them tea when they are on yard duty and give them an apple each day. Very rare. No one has ever been awarded this order.

Knights today

Today in Britain 'knight' is just a title given by the government to pop stars, sportsmen, government servants … and anyone rich enough to pay for a 'knighthood'. A couple of million pounds should do it.

You don't even need a horse or a sword and you don't have to fight for the queen … you just need a very big pot of money.

King Edward II would be annoyed that all the glory has gone. I bet he'd swell up with rage and bust his garter.

Warrior kings

Early English kings were the number-one knights in the country. What do you know about these Middle Ages monarchs?

Just answer 'True' or 'False' and see if you are a lion-heart or a lame-brain.

Knight Out magazine
❖ Know Your Nobles Quiz ❖

1 Edward I (1239–1307) cheated by flying false flags in a battle. True or false?

2 King Edward III (1312–77) had a round table made for his knights. True or false?

3 King Richard III (ruled 1483–85) died crying, 'A horse! A horse! My kingdom for a horse!' True or false?

4 Henry V (1387–1422) ordered his men to murder their French prisoners. True or false?

5 King Henry II (1133–89) ate straw when a knight praised his enemy. True or false?

6 King John (ruled 1299–1316) signed a great charter (the Magna Carta) to stop his knights rebelling. True or false?

7 Richard I (ruled 1189–99) spent 17 months as a prisoner in a castle. His faithful minstrel, Blondel, set off to search for him. He sat outside the walls of castles and sang Richard's favourite tune. Then, one day, he heard the King join in! He had found his lord. True or false?

8 King Edward I (1239–1307) ordered that, after his death, his body should be boiled and his bones carried into battles against the Scots. True or false?

9 Alfred the Great (849–901) once hid in a peasant's house without telling the woman who he was. She asked him to look after the cakes in her oven. He was so busy working on his bow that he let the cakes burn. The woman gave him a good telling off without realizing she was speaking to her king. True/False?

10 Henry VII (ruled 1485–1509) defeated Richard III at Bosworth in 1485 then gave him a fine funeral and a tomb in Westminster Abbey. True or false?

Answers:

1) True. Edward was accused of being a bit of a cheat in the 1265 Battle of Evesham. He captured some banners from one of the enemy barons and flew them over his own army. So, of course, the other enemy barons didn't attack him. When he was close enough he showed his true colours -- and attacked them. Their leader, Simon de Montfort, was captured and beheaded.

2) True. Edward pinched the idea from the legends about King Arthur's Round Table. King Arthur's Round Table was a folk-tale -- Edward's was fact. You can still see it in the Great Hall of Winchester Castle.

3) False. He cries that in the play *Richard III* by William Shakespeare. But in real life (or real death) he probably cried 'Ouch! Get that sword out of my head'.

4) True. At the Battle of Agincourt (1415) the English took a lot of French prisoners. They were sent to the back of the English army. Then there was a fresh French attack. Henry was worried that the prisoners would join in and attack him from the back. He ordered that all the French prisoners should be put to death.

5) True. One day a knight was stupid enough to say something in praise of William the Lion, King of Scotland. William was Henry II's deadliest enemy. Henry was so enraged, one historian said...

GRR

Henry flung his cap from his head, pulled off his belt, threw off his cloak and clothes, grabbed the silk cover off the couch and started chewing pieces of straw.

6) False. King John put his royal seal on the Magna Carta when his bad barons bullied him. But he DIDN'T sign it … because King John couldn't write.

7) False. It's a nice story but it was almost certainly made up by minstrels to make a minstrel look like a hero!

8) True. He ORDERED that … but it never happened. When Edward died his son refused to dunk dad in the boiling pot.

9) False. The story was first told 300 years after Alfred died.

10) False. Richard was buried in an unmarked grave and we don't know where it is now. His stone coffin was paid for by Henry VII. But there is a story that the coffin was dug up and turned into a horse trough for many years. Later it was broken up to make steps for a pub cellar.

☠ DID YOU KNOW…? ☠

If a knight wanted his son to grow up as a knight he would give the baby its first feed from the tip of his sword. (Don't try this at home with baby brothers.)

Epilogue

In 1876 a group of US soldiers on horseback attacked a camp of Native American Indians at the Little Big Horn River in Dakota.

It was a daft thing to do. They were badly led by General George Custer and they were poor soldiers. They made a last stand on a hilltop and their enemies rode round and picked them off one by one.

Custer's US Cavalry troop were wiped out. The Sioux Indians killed every one.

It was a stupid waste of life.

But Custer's Last Stand went down in history as a glorious battle.

Why? Because there's something wild and exciting about men riding horses in a wild charge.

Bloodthirsty knights in armour or dimwit US cavalry, cruel conquistadors or carving Cossacks will always be remembered as heroes. People will usually forget the savage fighting and the blood they spilt – the enemy blood and their own blood.

The truth is they WERE horrible. Riding at people and slicing or hacking, shooting or smashing is really a bad idea.

Interesting Index

Hang on! This isn't one of your boring old indexes. This is a horrible index. It's the only index in the world where you will find 'backside wiping', 'dog-poo', 'horse-flesh soup' and all the other things you really HAVE to know if you want to be a horrible historian. Read it and creep.